WARNING

This book contains sexually explicit scenes and adult language. It may be considered offensive to some readers. This book is for sale to adults ONLY.

* * * * * * * * * * * * * * * * * * *

Please store your files wisely where they cannot be accessed by underage readers.

Other Books by Darla Dunbar:

<u>The Romeo Alpha BBW Paranormal Shifter Romance Series</u>

Amanda Walker thinks that she has a normal and boring life. That is until after her 24th birthday. Everything changes when she meets the man who says he was supposed to be her husband. Denying everything the man says, she fights him every step of the way. But after he kidnaps her, Amanda discovers that there are some things about her family that her parents kept a secret all these years. Among the history of the family she learns secrets she thought only happened in story books. Can Amanda tell the difference between truth and lies or is she this mysterious woman that holds the key to a legacy?

<u>Romeo Alpha Blood Lines Romance Series</u>

Twenty-four years have passed in relative peace for Amanda and Romeo. They've raised five children into adulthood and are thoroughly enjoying their lives as the Alpha King and Queen of the werewolves. At twenty-four, Sarina is just stepping into her powers and will be ripe for mating when her birthday comes in two weeks. What no one knows is the danger that lurks just outside their tight knit community. Romeo has made peace with the other clans and has enjoyed that peace, but it will all come crashing down around him when his oldest daughter comes of age to take a mate.

<u>The Alpha Feud BBW Paranormal Shifter Romance Series</u>

Eliza's life consisted of reporting on boring, crowd-pleasing events, like their country livestock fair. With the arrival of two handsome brothers, the lives of Eliza and her best friend, Melissa, are shaken to the core. For Eliza, the arrival of this new man becomes a test of her relationship with her current boyfriend, who she's been happily living with for over six years. Does Hayden, a complete stranger, really wield the power to make Eliza reconsider her relationship with Andrew?

<u>The Alpha Packed BBW Paranormal Shifter Romance Series</u>

Darlene has led a quiet life since suffering through a terrible break-up. She wants nothing more than to spend her time in front of the TV, away from any sort of trouble. But all that goes down the drain when handsome, rugged and rough Idris comes into her life. He is a werewolf on the lookout for his missing pack leader. Darlene quickly finds herself pulled towards this mysterious man and at the same time finds herself falling deeper and deeper into the world of the supernatural.

<u>The Daemon Paranormal Romance Chronicles</u>

The daemon infighting can only be stopped when a strong leader emerges to calm the different factions. Juno appears to be at the heart of the conflict. Things become complicated when Phoebe and Supay try to negotiate with the siren, Juno. The love triangle among Phoebe, Supay and Apollo become tense when Juno's meddling threatens to destroy any romance that develops.

<u>The Leather Satchel Paranormal Romance Series</u>

Valtina is stuck in Middle World, unable to pass on to The Afterlife. In order to redeem herself from past deeds done, she must help bring romance back into the world and stop The Dark Side from destroying love in its entirety. Following orders issued by Ladaya and armed with a leather satchel filled with the appropriate tools and weapons, Valtina embraces each mission with enthusiasm.

Get the latest update on new releases from the author at:

https://darladunbar.com/newsletter/

This book is Part One of the "<u>The Mind Talker Paranormal Romance Series</u>"

Book 1 - Awareness

Ananda discovered that she can read other people's mind when she was 11. It is supposed to be a gift but it's driving her crazy. Lonely and disoriented, Ananda runs off to New York. She thinks that in a city as big as that, there must be someone like her walking around. One day, man's voice calls out to her. The strange thing is that she heard the voice in her mind.

Book 2 - Hunted

Jared's past haunted him and served as a reminder that he can't escape his fate. If he had stopped the boy back then, would his sister still be alive? Jenny was the love of Jared's life until he discovered she was living a double life. Jenny was part of a secret organization that was bent on hunting him.

Book 3 - Heat

Ananda couldn't help herself. Jared's scent just sends her over the edge. No one else understood Ananda's gift... not even her parents. When Jared found Ananda, he explained what her special powers meant. Only certain people acquired the gift of reading minds. Along with that, Ananda was undergoing a maturation process. Every one of her kind will experience it in their 21st year.

Book 4 - Revealed

Jared learns the truth about his dead sister. Ananda had the power to see into his past. She saw what he saw during that fateful day when Jared's sister died. Meanwhile, the truth about Kerri's family is revealed. They are the sole reason why Ananda and her kind are on the endangered list.

Book 5 - Evasion

Ryan is the mystery man who is helping Jared and Ananda to escape to Canada in hopes of evading the organization that is hunting all those with special mind reading powers. Kerri's family is behind the secret organization. Her love for Ryan has forced her to choose between loyalty to family and loyalty to Ryan. Can she be trusted?

The Mind Talker Paranormal Romance Series

Awareness

Book One

By Darla Dunbar

Copyright Revelry Publishing 2015

Table of Contents

Chapter One

"SO SEXY…"

"God I'd love to do her…"

"I wonder if I could find that outfit in my size…"

Ananda had to fight laughter, curling an errant lock of dark auburn hair around her finger as she fought through the crowd of people around her. Laughing for no reason, at least none that could be seen by the general population, is typically frowned upon and usually makes finding friends much more difficult. This she had learned the hard way thanks to the cruelty of middle school students and their need to be popular. Still, it never ceased to surprise her how many inane thoughts humans regularly had running through their minds. Sometimes, Ananda had to totally isolate herself in order to get a moment's rest, particularly when surrounded by the chatter from all directions. Her honey-colored eyes flitted back and forth as she scanned the mass of people around her, thoughts flying into her mind in rapid succession.

It wasn't like Ananda couldn't turn it off, her ability to hear other people's thoughts. When she was younger, it was definitely more difficult to sift through the roiling voices and images that seemed to seep into her head with little direction or effort. At first when her ability manifested at the tender age of eleven, Ananda was terrified as were her parents, who were ignorant of such abilities. Her older brother Ryan had been a source of strength and stability for her as the family went from one psychologist to another attempting to find a reason or cure for the 'voices' Ananda claimed to hear. It was he, who helped her find a center in order to control the flow of voices until they were barely more than a brush against her mind. Ryan's move across the country for school was rough though manageable for Ananda as she began to explore the range of her ability and discover the fun she could have with it. Her moral compass wasn't as low as some, so she didn't use it for anything that would get her ahead academically, but she did use it to benefit herself and those she loved.

"Ananda, over here!"

Refocusing on the crowd around her, Ananda spotted one of the few people she could actually call a friend. Kerri wasn't what anyone would call quiet. Her small stature and pixie-like features made it seem as if she could be blown away by a single puff of air, but her exuberant personality and sharp, sometimes biting, use of sarcasm made her seem larger than her thin frame. Bright red hair the color of the sunset and eyes that seemed to change color depending on her mood completed the full package that was Kerri Donahue. However, it wasn't just Kerri's larger-than-life personality that drew Ananda in, it was more of what Kerri didn't exude. Her mind was quiet.

No matter how intently Ananda poked and prodded, she could only get a faint hum and vague feelings from her friend's mind. Rather than being unnerved by that, Ananda felt a sense of relief at finally finding one person who didn't give her a headache just by being around so often. Even with her brother Ryan, Ananda had to occasionally leave in order to calm her own mind and get some relief from his mind's 'voice.' The fact that Kerri seemed oblivious to how special she was sometimes made Ananda pause and wonder if she was the only one out there with a strange ability. Was there someone out there like Professor X who was searching for people like her? Was there a way to find others? Or did she spend way too much time reading comic books and hoping that some parts of those stories were influenced by actual facts?

Chapter Two

In the nine years since Ananda discovered her ability to read minds, not once had she ever come across anyone who seemed to be able to do the same. She had tried going to palm readers and calling so-called psychics, but so far they had all been scams. Their own minds would betray their lack of abilities sometimes before Ananda had even handed over her money. She had decided upon going to NYU with the vague hope that in a city as crowded as New York, there would be at least one other person who shared in her ability that she could commiserate with. After two years of hoping and searching, she had grown discouraged and until meeting Kerri, Ananda had even considered moving back home to Phoenix and abandoning her search altogether. Meeting the other girl had been soothing to her soul and Ananda felt renewed enough to continue her search for others like her; she had even decided to expand her search overseas.

As soon as Ananda was close enough, Kerri linked their arms beaming up at her with a beatific smile. Ananda couldn't hear anything, but she could sense a general feeling of comfort emanating from the shorter girl.

"So I was thinking. After this farce of a homecoming game," Kerri sneered at the direction of the scoreboard, "Perhaps we should hit up the quad and do a little man-hunting. It's been way too long since I got any action and I know for a fact that you haven't had anything between your legs that didn't require batteries for far longer."

Ananda couldn't help her snort of laughter. It was true that she had been experiencing a bit of a dry spell for the past few months though she wasn't a prude by any means. Sex had always been fun, even though most people seemed to have the same mantra running through their heads.

"Don't stop…more…"

"Feels so good…"

"Yes…"

There were a few times where she was surprised by thoughts of violence, though they had never physically manifested with her, thankfully. And still there were rare moments when it seemed as if the other person could read Ananda's mind. She would be thinking about a move one of her previous partners had done and the new one would do it. Or if she were enjoying one particular position and her partner was about to change it, they would jerk as if shocked by something and change their mind. Sometimes Ananda wondered if perhaps she had other powers and abilities that she was just unaware of.

"…just better than any guy I've ever met!" Kerri finished with a high little squeal bringing Ananda's attention back to their conversation.

"Who?"

Kerri paused to look at her friend. "Did you hear anything I just said?"

"I heard the part about sex and my vibrator and then something about more sex…possibly with a guy…" Ananda shrugged as her voice trailed off. Truthfully, she didn't really want to know what her friend was talking about. Sex for her had gotten stale and boring and until she meets someone amazing, Ananda doubted she would feel inclined to do something about her lack of sexual partners for the past few months. "Honestly, I just haven't been in the mood for anything with anyone." She smiled and leaned into Kerri, bumping their shoulders together. "I'll just have to live vicariously through you and perhaps sleep with my ear against the wall."

Ananda smiled as she watched her friend laugh uproariously.

"I'll try to be extra noisy just for you my friend. But first I need to scope out the competition." Kerri turned to survey the crowd leaving Ananda free to scan the voices coming at her from all sides.

"So fake. I can't believe she did that!"

"If he doesn't propose I'm leaving!"

"I really hate her…"

"…Ananda…"

Startled, Ananda jerked in place as though she were slapped. She could hear Kerri still discussing the merits of one guy over another, but the sound of that deep voice saying her name had her attention. It wasn't the first time she had heard her name in someone's thoughts, but it was the first time that it felt as if it were meant for her alone. Trying not to be obvious, Ananda scanned the crowd hoping to spot the person behind the thought. Everywhere she saw people utterly focused on the game; no one so much as glanced in her direction.

"…and that guy looks like a serial killer or child molester or something. Like, didn't anyone ever tell him that those mustaches are just not attractive? I mean think about that in bed, the whole…"

"…I know you can hear me…Ananda…"

It was unnerving. As much as Ananda had desired to find someone like her, now that the moment was here she found herself wanting to run. Something inside of her was repulsed by the idea of someone else being able to see inside of her mind and she quickly put up a barrier in her mind. She could feel Kerri tense up and wondered again if her friend had abilities she just wasn't yet aware of.

"Are you okay, Ana?" The concern in Kerri's voice was so thick it was almost physical. Ananda felt the desire to wrap herself in it like a child burrowing into his mother for comfort.

"I…" She could feel another brush against her mind as if someone were asking for permission to enter. "I'm not feeling very well. I think I want to head back to the apartment." Unhooking her arm, Ananda forced herself to appear calm so as not to draw any unwanted attention to herself. It was difficult with the overwhelming amount of concern her friend was radiating. It hadn't been this hard for Ananda to block out the feelings of others in a long time and if not for Kerri's naivety she might have actually snapped at the girl.

"What's wrong? Should I go with you?" Kerri reached out in an attempt to grab Ananda's wrist, but she paused as if sensing that somehow it would be the wrong move to make. Once again, Kerri's attentiveness the minute Ananda's demeanor changes was surprising. Only Ryan had ever been able to read Ananda once she learned to block her own thoughts and feelings. Normally she would feel grateful that her friend was so attentive, but at this moment, it just made her feel even more cornered, as if she were the prey in a fight for survival.

"Ananda…relax…" That voice in her mind, she couldn't be completely sure but it sounded so familiar to her. Almost as if she had heard it in a dream. She tried to calm her mind while continuing to discreetly scan her surroundings. She was a bit worried that if the guy was good enough to penetrate her mind's defenses, that he would be more than skilled enough to hide the fact that he was broadcasting his thoughts to her in the first place.

Turning back to Kerri, Ananda forced a semi-sincere smile on her face in an attempt to placate her friend's concern. "Nah, I'm fine. I'm just going to go back and put on some PJs and relax with a book…nonacademic, I promise." Ananda was quick to add after seeing the thunderous look on Kerri's face.

"Good! I've been telling you for months that you've been working too hard. Go relax, take a bubble bath or something." Laughing, Kerri pushed Ananda back towards the way she came. Her kaleidoscope eyes still had lingering concern, but she gave a small smile for reassurance. Ananda stopped for a moment and really looked at her friend. For some reason she felt as if this would be the last time she would be able to see her friend for a long while, and for a moment she contemplated ignoring the voice in her head and wrapping herself in the cloak of safety Kerri always seemed to exude.

"You're right," Ananda replied, pausing to pull her friend into a much-needed embrace. She let the scent of Kerri's strawberry shampoo wash over her as if committing it to memory. "I love you, Ker." Pulling away quickly, Ananda hurried off, without a backward glance. She knew if she looked back at her friend, she would be unable to do anything but clutch at the smaller girl. Perhaps if she knew what was waiting for her, she may have looked back after all.

The trek back across campus was a little disconcerting for Ananda. On one hand, there were still people milling about, laughing about the lousy game or enjoying a drink or two with friends. A few times Ananda was stopped by someone she knew from class or the few nights she deigned to do anything other than study in the library. The entire journey back to her apartment, she couldn't quite shake the feeling of being watched, as if someone was just waiting to materialize from the shadows. The feeling put her on the edge and more than once, Ananda found herself peering intently into the shadows, listening for the voice which had so unnerved her previously. Was the person still at the game? Did she know them? Surely she didn't just imagine everything; she was gifted, not crazy. But why after all this time was the person coming out to her now? And why did the voice sound so damn familiar? These were thoughts and questions that could only be answered when she found the person who called to her.

Chapter Three

Ananda crossed the street as her apartment came into view. Out of habit, she glanced up at the window of the apartment she and Kerri shared and was alarmed to see it illuminated. She could have sworn that they turned out all of the lights before they left. Had Kerri decided to come home early as well? Slowing her walk, Ananda reached out with her mind, confusion spiking when she brushed across something cold and wholly unfamiliar. Just then she could see a figure moving in the hallway, almost into view. Something inside her began to freeze at the thought that the person in her apartment was there for a far more sinister reason than just talking, and she found herself frozen in place with panic. The figure moved even closer to the window and Ananda knew that if she didn't get a hold of herself then she would easily be spotted standing alone on the sidewalk.

"Move!"

The thought burst through her mind's defenses as one hand gripped her wrist and another covered her wide stretched mouth. She was dragged into a narrow alley between two buildings and found herself struggling against someone with far more strength than her 120-pound frame possessed.

"Breathe…quiet. We don't want to be felt, otherwise we're both dead. Understood?"

The person behind her tightened their grip and Ananda nodded once briefly to convey that she understood. Despite being pulled into an alley by a stranger whose size and stature far dwarfed her own, Ananda felt surprisingly calm. She did what the stranger said and focused on breathing slowly and silently through her nose. She was intrigued to find a scent, cloying and sweet like honey, that seemed to be emanating from somewhere in their vicinity. An answering scent, musky with a citrus tint, seemed to unfurl around her and she jolted when she realized that the smell was coming from the person still holding her so closely in the middle of a dark alley. She wondered if the man knew his scent was so enticing and if it was a brand of cologne that she could buy in order to have it covering her always.

As if sensing the direction her thoughts had gone in and how little of a flight risk Ananda really was, the man behind her slowly peeled his hand away from her mouth and brought it down to clutch at her hip. A shiver of electricity seemed to travel from the stranger's fingers directly into Ananda's suddenly oversensitive skin, and she could feel him tense.

"Stop it…"

Despite not being able to see the man, Ananda could tell that he was scowling, gaze sharp on the back of her neck even as his errant fingers began softly stroking the sensitive skin of her hip. Just that little contact seemed to ignite a flood of pleasure in Ananda's body, the strength of which she had never before felt. It was as if her body had been put on pause until this very moment, a fateful meeting.

"Wait."

Turning her head slightly, Ananda caught a small glimpse of the man behind the haunting voice. She was momentarily taken aback by the sharp cut of cheekbones that trickled down into a sculpted jaw covered with dark, day-old stubble. The top half of his face was still shadowed, but she knew his attention was still focused on the apartment light that shouldn't be on. Trying to focus on the situation at hand, Ananda turned her gaze back to the direction of her apartment. She couldn't see the window from where they were hidden, but she somehow knew that even the slightest movement would give up their location in the dark. She forced herself to mentally relax and focused on making her mind as clear and see-through as possible.

"Good, you're doing good…"

The praise from the dark stranger made Ananda practically purr, and she tried to distract her mind from the desire to turn around and grasp that chin before attacking what was sure to be a sinfully decadent mouth. No one's inner voice could be that sensual without there being some outward evidence of it. The man's scent was still wrapped around her and without thinking, she took a long drag in as if to embed it into her nostrils permanently. She wondered how she smelled to the man after being surrounded by so many people earlier. As if reading her thoughts, the man's head came forward and he nosed behind the shell of her ear. Ananda could feel the hair on the back of her neck stirring with each breath the man took and she hoped that he found her scent as mesmerizing and intriguing as she found his. For some reason, she wasn't concerned about why she could so clearly pick out the aroma of the still silent man over the pungent smell of trash.

"Who are you?" Ananda whispered as quietly as she could without drawing attention to anyone who happened to walk by. It wouldn't necessarily be a good thing to get caught in an alley at night with a strange man who may or may not be a serial killer. Though the fact that all he had really done was hold her and sniff behind her ear made Ananda less inclined to think of the man as a killer. Then again, wasn't it always the quiet ones you had to look out for? "Are you going to like, kidnap me and cut me into little pieces or something?"

The man tensed for a moment before his shoulders began shaking up and down. His breath huffed out beside Ananda's ear and she could tell the man was laughing at her. Before she could get worked up enough to demand answers, she was jolted by the man's gravelly voice.

"Jared."

Chapter Four

Swallowing reflexively, Ananda tried not to tremble. "Jared. Okay. Great name. So, how about my other question?" The man stopped his quiet laughter and once again tensed behind her. "Are you planning on killing me?"

"…No."

Relaxing, Ananda tried again to see the man's face fully. "So what are you going to do with me then? Why are you here? Who the hell is in my apartment? Why is someone…" Ananda trailed off from her incessant questioning as a familiar hum brushed against her mind. "Kerri!" Jerking her gaze back to the street, Ananda almost threw herself out of the alley at the sight of her friend walking up to their apartment building. If not for Jared's sturdy grip she would have been halfway down the sidewalk before consciously considering her actions.

"Quiet!" Jared hissed tightening his hold once again. The hand that had been gripping her hip once again came up to muffle the enraged sounds tumbling from Ananda's mouth as she struggled to reach her friend. She was terrified. There was an unknown intruder in their apartment whose very aura was enough to scare Ananda without even trying, and her unsuspecting friend was being led like a lamb to the slaughter.

"Calm down and stay quiet!" Jared's inner voice was practically growling at her with impatience, the fury of it enough to bring tears to Ananda's eyes. "I will keep your friend safe. Just trust me and calm the fuck down!" Swallowing down a sob, Ananda forced her eyes to follow her best friend's path and was startled to see the lithe girl pause in the middle of the sidewalk with a look of barely contained confusion. It seemed as if Kerri couldn't make up her mind what to do for a moment before nodding and turning back the way she came. Ananda's state of shock was so great that she didn't realize Jared had begun leading her back towards a car he had stashed on the other side of the alley. It wasn't until they were moving steadily away from her apartment building that Ananda seemed to remember she had been practically kidnapped by some unknown stranger, and she turned to finally take in the man.

His day-old stubble looked just as inky black as it had in the alley and Ananda could see he had thick eyebrows of the same midnight hue. His hair was lush and thick with a slight curl that made her want to run her hands through to feel if it was as soft as it appeared. Broad muscular shoulders were barely even contained in a tight black Henley that screamed criminal, but those weren't even his best feature. No, that would be his eyes, ice blue and glinting like diamonds. Ananda could tell that this man had been through some unimaginable situations though he looked like he was roughly around her own age. She wondered what more he knew about these abilities and how he had managed to get Kerri to turn from danger with just a thought. Her mind was such a rolling mess of confusion and half-formed questions that their abrupt pull into a motel off the side of the highway barely made a blip on her mind's radar until she found herself in an unfamiliar room perched on the edge of a really uncomfortable mattress.

Ananda blinked slowly up at Jared who stood in front of a window peering into the darkness of the night as if looking for something. "What is going on Jared? Why did you bring me here and who are we running from?" Ananda was almost startled by how breathless she sounded, but the still present scent of the man in front of her was still wreaking havoc on her senses. Surely the man could tell the effect he was having on her?

"And why do you smell so good?"

Jared jolted away from the window and fixed an intense stare on Ananda. "I smell good? You have no idea how difficult it was for me to hold still in that alley." He walked slowly over to the bed until he was so close that Ananda was forced to tilt her head up at an awkward angle to maintain eye contact. The temperature in the room seemed to jump a couple of degrees and Ananda could feel her skin begin to moisten with sweat. Unconsciously, she licked her lips and her eyes widened as she saw piercing blue eyes hone in on that small unconscious movement. Without thinking, Ananda reached up and ran a soft finger across Jared's brow before placing the offending digit in her mouth and closing her eyes with a groan. How was it possible for sweat to taste so sweet? She could hear Jared's breathing become labored and she shivered with the knowledge that she was affecting him as much as she herself was affected.

When Ananda opened her eyes, Jared was gazing down at her face, positioned like he was expecting her to go running and screaming into the night. Strangely enough, she had no such thoughts other than getting everything she could from this man, right there and then. Scooting back on the bed, Ananda flung herself back hitting the two small pillows that they had before pushing them to the side. She wiggled a little to get comfortable while raising both arms over her head and arching her back. It was the first time she had consciously used her physical body only to entice another person. The way Jared's eyes seemed to darken as they trailed down her prone body made her think that perhaps she should try it more often.

Jared's gaze zeroed in on the small sliver of skin where her shirt had been lifted with her arm movement. Stalking her onto the bed, he leaned his face down to nuzzle and mouth at that stretch of skin igniting nerves in Ananda's body that she had previously been wholly unaware of. She had been turned on ever since first being pulled into the alley and her core was starting to ache with the need to be taken and repeatedly filled. Never before had a partner solicited such a response from her as if their bodies were being magnetically pulled to one another. It didn't look as if Jared was much better off, a sizeable bulge clearly visible in the dark jeans he was wearing. Still, he hadn't moved beyond nuzzling her stomach and Ananda was beginning to wonder if perhaps she was just dreaming. "Jared?"

The man finally looked up, eyes burning with so much clear desire and such hunger that Ananda couldn't stop the whine that pushed past her throat. Never had a man looked at her with so much need and it made her question all of the sexual encounters she had had before. Slowly as if not to startle her, Jared moved closer, eyes still fastened to the reddened skin of her lips. Ananda leaned up those last few inches in order to bring their mouths together in their first kiss.

What started out as a slow exploration quickly turned into a torrid affair of bitten lips and thrusting tongues. Ananda couldn't stop the sounds tumbling from her lips as she gasped and sucked on Jared's upper lip. His hands were like hot brands running up and down the sides of her body, shirt being pushed further and further up with each pass until the bulk of it was tucked into her under arm. Sinful fingers slid up to brush maddeningly soft and then skin-scorching harder circles against her upturned nipples. Ananda's bra was pushed underneath her ample bosom as Jared's lips migrated down to suck and nip at first one and then the other in quick succession. Ananda found she could do little more than arch and gasp as her nerves came alive, goosebumps popping up like wildfire on her overheated skin. She squirmed until she got one of her legs free in order to plant one foot on the mattress, knees spread wide enough for Jared to settle between. She could feel the hard heat of his manhood pushing against the fabric of her shorts and Ananda found herself angry at the thought of anything between them.

"Off," she said hoarsely, and shoved at Jared's shirt until he leaned away from her sensitized nipples in order to pull the offending garment off. The moment he was free, he dove down, tongue tangling with hers in an obscene parody of what their bodies would soon be doing. It was like Jared would die if he didn't get more of her mouth and tongue. Ananda was finding herself distracted by the breadth of Jared's back, the heated warmth of his skin and the way he shuddered when she scratched her nails down his spine. Suddenly Ananda knew what that cloying honey sweet scent was. It was her!

Her body had been reacting to Jared's since the moment they came in contact and his had been responding in turn. Now the air was full of the smell of pheromones released with every bump and grind of their bodies. Despite this, Ananda had no intention of stopping until she was sated. She bucked her hips up into his in an effort to show him she was ready to get down to the main event. Detaching her hands from his wide back, Ananda slid them down to grasp at the buttons to Jared's jeans. He made a hoarse noise in her ear as he leaned back letting her peal the zipper down and pull out his quickly hardening cock. The sight of him made her mouth water with the desire to feel that heavy heat on her tongue. She got a few enthusiastic strokes in before Jared was twisting out of her grasp and backing up and away from the bed. He kicked off his jeans and underwear and Ananda couldn't help but gaze hungrily at the man in all his toned naked glory.

Sculpted abs and pecs led down to a happy trail that made Ananda's fingers itch to tangle with. Jared's cock was a thing of beauty, hard and weeping slightly with the evidence of his desire. He gave her a moment to stare before reaching for her again to help Ananda out of her shorts. When she made a move to remove her panties he stopped her by simply angling them out of the way, eyes focused on her hidden depths.

"How far do you want this to go Ana?" It was the first thing either of them had said in a while, and Ananda startled, not expecting the question or the familiar nickname. Jared was sitting back balanced on his haunches and Ananda suddenly knew without a doubt that if she said it, Jared would be content with just kissing and frottage for the night. Leaning up to wrap her arm around his neck, Ananda pulled the man on top of her and reached down with the other in order to line his cock up with her pulsating core.

"Everything. Give me everything, Jared."

The sound of his name must have been more than the man could handle, because without another word he drove into her, slickened walls ensuring his smooth entry. Though it had been months since Ananda had last been with anyone, the abrupt and quick entry gave her nothing but toe curling pleasure and she didn't think twice about wrapping her legs around Jared's torso. She could feel the muscles in his back as he surged into her over and over again, the sound of skin meeting startlingly loud in the otherwise quiet room. Their lips met, though it was less of a kiss and more of breathing in one another's air as gasps and moans were shared back and forth. Ananda could feel her body clenching with the need for release and she gripped Jared's ass in an attempt to push him deeper inside of her. Sweat slickened her brow as she tossed her head back and forth in an effort to stave off her release. As if knowing her predicament, Jared pushed himself even harder, cock brushing against her core and setting off an explosion of fireworks behind her eyelids. But it was inevitable that the end would be reached and as she heard his familiar voice inside of her head, Ananda's body snapped into an arch, every muscle tightening with release.

"Come for me…"

Distantly Ananda could hear Jared's groan as her body pushed him into his own climax, but she could do little more than breathe as her vision faded to black.

To be continued in Book 2

If you enjoyed this title, I would appreciate your leaving a review of the book. Good reviews encourage an author to write as well as help books to sell. Good reviews can be just a few short sentences describing what you liked about the book without having a spoiler. If you could spend 30 seconds writing a review, I would appreciate it: you can review this title right now at your favorite retailer.

Here is a preview of the **next story** you may enjoy:

Hunted - The Mind Talker Paranormal Romance Series, Book 2

WAKING UP was an experience for Jared. It had been years since he had felt an inkling of the comfort that is sleeping wrapped around someone he didn't have to worry about stabbing him in the back. It had been months since he last let his guard down enough to be intimate with anyone other than himself.

And yet this girl, someone who had never even been properly informed of what they were, had somehow blown clear past all of his defenses before he even realized they were down. It gave him an uneasy feeling the fact that he responded to her so quickly. He had thought himself incapable of feeling anything for another person other than hate and mistrust after all he had been through.

Jared's life wasn't rough in the beginning. He grew up in a normal household, with normal parents, a normal older sister and a normal dog. Overall his early life was completely and utterly normal. And then came puberty.

His freshman year of high school brought the normal bouts of acne and anger indicative of a boy on the journey of becoming a man. Being the nerd that he originally was, he had read every article and book on the subject that he could get his grubby little hands on, including some not so hidden Playboys that his dad kept stashed in a cooler in the garage. Everything that he had been experiencing was so tragically normal that it was almost a relief when he started hearing the voices. At first he thought himself crazy, maybe mad like the hatter from Alice and Wonderland; until the voices began to sound familiar. He could make out his sister's voice, shrill and lively even when muted. Then it was his parents. Soon he was hearing every thought contained in his high school and he realized what real crazy was.

It was a chilly day in November, the day before Thanksgiving break ironically, when one of his classmates, a boy who had been picked on and bullied for years and who Jared had been close acquaintances with moving in similar social circles, decided that he couldn't handle the pressure anymore. Jared had known that the boy, Kevin, was unstable just by listening to his rather disturbing thoughts day in and day out. He could hear the boy plotting something big, something that would stop his never-ending pain. Jared had known all this and yet he had done nothing. He was still getting a handle on control and though the boy's thoughts were filled with darkness, on the outside he appeared put together and in control. Jared feared that at best no one would believe him and at worst he'd put himself in harm's way if Kevin decided to take out his anger on him. So Jared stayed quiet, never even telling his sister, who was in the year above him, his concerns.

Jared had been sitting out on the lacrosse field where he normally took his lunch so he could avoid any awkwardness in the school cafeteria. His sister had often offered him a seat with her friends, but he usually turned her down in favor of his solo spot. It wasn't that he was anti-social, it's just that he knew one day he would grow into his looks and be, if not attractive, then at least average. However, he didn't want to sit for forty-five minutes and hear his sister's harpy friends with their high-pitched inner voices squawking and gushing over it. He thought that people who said women mature faster than men were horribly misinformed and probably home-schooled.

It was for this very reason that Jared heard rather than saw the commotion that happened without any warning. One minute he was biting into an apple, geometry book balanced on one knee, and the next he found himself sprawled on his side with his ears ringing as his lungs fought to pull in air. All around he could see bits of rock and drywall lying beside him and for one minute he wondered if he was dreaming. Slowly he started to make out the sounds of screams over his groans as he pushed his body up into a seated position. The scene that unfolded before him was straight out of a war movie.

If you enjoyed this sample then look for **Hunted - The Mind Talker Paranormal Romance Series, Book 2**.

Here is a preview of **another story** you may enjoy:

**The Awakening: The Daemon Paranormal
Romance Chronicles, Book 1**

THE LAST customer of the day was slowly leaving. Phoebe reached down to pet her dog, Ace, and moved to close up shop. Since graduating high school, she had worked in fairs across the country as a fortune teller, saving money. She did not know why, but when she touched somebody's hand, she could read their thoughts. Although she could not divine their future, she could make educated guesses that were enough to bring customers back. After saving enough money, she had finally opened up her own shop.

Removing the scarf from around her hair, Phoebe let her red curls cascade along her shoulders. Ace sniffed at some of his dog food while she reached over to grab her purse. Before she could close up, a knock at the door surprised her. In front of the door, she saw one of the most gorgeous men she had ever laid eyes on. Curious, she opened the door and let him in.

"Hello! How can I help you, Mr...?" She paused and waited for him to respond.

"My name is Apollo Mikos. Pleasure to meet you, Phoebe Williams." The blonde-haired man reached for her hand and shook it. Instantly, a vision arose before her eyes of Apollo and her rolling around in bed sheets. Waves crashed outside the window—a storm was brewing. As the vision of Apollo entered her body forcefully, Phoebe pulled her hand back. The vision went away, but it left a slight blush on Phoebe's cheeks. Reading the minds of other people was occasionally embarrassing and often felt like a major invasion of privacy. Still, she found herself wishing that she could have held his hand a little longer to see where these thoughts took her.

Motioning toward the table and chairs reserved for clients, she asked if he wanted to sit down. Apollo just shook his head.

"I need your help with something, but not like that." He shrugged his shoulders. Tall and well-built, Apollo had blue eyes and chiseled features. He wore a dark black suit that made all of his muscles ripple beneath the fabric.

Confused, Phoebe looked over at him. "What do you mean?"

Sighing, Apollo looked into her eyes. "You will probably want to sit down for this." Still uncertain, Phoebe sat down and waited for him to speak again.

Gazing out the window, Apollo framed his thoughts. "I know your mother, Rhea. I also know what you really are and I need your help."

Phoebe was aghast. "What do you mean? I don't have a mother. I grew up in foster care after my mother left me there when I was two."

If you enjoyed this sample then look for **The Awakening: The Daemon Paranormal Romance Chronicles, Book 1**.

Here is a preview of **another story** you may enjoy:

Alpha Packed: A BBW Paranormal Shifter Romance - Book 1

THIS WAS a huge mistake. Darlene should have known better, but in utter and total desperation, she agreed to this date. Now the guy in front of her—what was his name again? Steve? Mike? She couldn't even remember now—had been talking non-stop about pro wrestling. But not even actual real wrestling. The stuff that was fake and basically just soap operas with some terrible phony fights thrown in.

"So then the Ice Cube challenged The Man to a battle!"

"Wow, really?" Darlene replied, feigning interest on every possible level.

This was her mistake. She had been spending way too much time at home lately, curled up on the couch, binge watching reality television shows because they made her feel better about her boring life. Darlene would leave for work in the mornings, do eight hours at a boring local bookstore, come home, eat and watch TV. She also stayed up far later than any normal human should, which resulted in limited forms of social communication.

That was how Darlene ended up on some free dating website. She deleted most of the messages she got. They were mostly from guys who seemed to think of her as a sexual fetish instead of an actual human being. Getting messages from guys who were into her being overweight made her feel uncomfortable. Darlene either got disgusted looks or sexual lust over her size.

Both sucked. She had been about to delete her page for good when a guy who appeared to be normal messaged her. He hadn't made any gross comments about her size and even made her laugh once or twice with his messages. It had been eight months since her last relationship blew up in her face. *Why not try something different?* She decided to accept his date.

The guy was so boring that Darlene wished the restaurant would go up in flames so she could flee. She was flipping through her options on how to end the date early when he finally pushed his plate away.

"That was delicious," he said.

"Oh yeah. It was great," Darlene lied, thinking the potatoes were too dry for her liking.

The check came and the guy—what was his name!—made an effort to search for his wallet. *Oh here we go...*

"Oh man. I forgot my wallet at home!" he said with fake surprise.

"Yeah, yeah, I got it," she mumbled, slamming her debit card on the table.

It didn't take a genius to figure out this asshole had asked her out to throw her what he thought was a "pity date" and get a free meal out of her. He would probably go home to all his idiot friends and talk about how he gave the fat girl a date because he was just so nice. Darlene felt like punching him in the face.

She paid, and they walked out of the restaurant in silence. He escorted her to her car and then glanced around, as if checking so that no one could see him, before he tried to kiss her.

"Yeah," Darlene lifted up her hand to block him, "I don't think so. Thanks for nothing though, seriously."

The man scowled and before he could say something back, Darlene got into her car. She pulled out of the parking lot as quickly as she could, wanting to forget the entire terrible date.

What a mistake. What an absolute mistake. Not even just the date. The last couple years of her life had been a huge mistake. She wished she could travel back in time and re-do everything. The first thing she'd do would be to say a resounding *no* when Austin proposed to her.

Darlene pulled into her apartment complex five minutes later. She had picked a nearby restaurant so she could make a quick escape home if needed. She walked up to the second floor. The couple by the stairwell was fighting again. They were constantly screaming at each other over everything. Some nights, Darlene wanted to yell back at them to just break up. Other times, she wanted to tell them to make it work, because being alone was terrible.

She opened the front door of her apartment and glanced around. Her computer was on in one corner, and a few blankets were thrown on the couch for maximum comfort for those times when she drowned herself in ice cream and terrible reality shows.

Everything else was clean though. Darlene couldn't stand her apartment being messy or dirty. She wanted it to be perfect, as if she could make her apartment look like how she didn't feel.

Darlene yanked off her high heels and plopped down in front of her computer. She deleted the online dating profile and stared out the window. That was it — she was going to become a hermit. Well, as much of a hermit as one can be if they still had to go to work and grocery shop and run errands…but other than that she was totally going to be a hermit from now on. People were not her thing. People were just terrible all around. And she'd had enough of terrible people.

She moved to the couch, wrapping herself up in a blanket. Darlene mused over what she would watch. Terrible shows about being tricked into online dating seemed like a good end to the night. It'd make her feel better at the very least.

Her cellphone rang loudly. Darlene jolted awake, startled. She wasn't used to her new ringtone. It used to be the theme song of an old cartoon she liked, but after everything went to hell she changed it to a normal ring in an effort to seem more adult. Now the ring was bleating loudly and annoying her. She looked at the front of the screen… her boss.

"Hello?"

"Hey, sorry, did I wake you?"

"No, Maria," Darlene lied. "What's up?"

"I had to fire Jacob. Can you cover his shift? You'd be working till three."

Darlene glanced at the clock to see it was a little past eight in the morning. "That's fine. I'll leave now."

She hopped in the shower, letting the warm water rush over her. She wasn't surprised that Maria had to fire Jacob. He was constantly late and unable to help any of the customers who came into the shop. The bookstore was small and dealt with books that couldn't be found at any of the chains. Business was slow, but the books were rare enough that Maria only needed to sell a few each month to keep the business going. Darlene liked how quiet it was and the fact that human interaction was minimal. She knew she needed to get over this slump she was in, but felt no desire to. Almost everything Darlene did as of late seemed to feed into it — her lifestyle, her job, even the stupid things she spent time watching and looking up online.

The bookstore was only a ten-minute drive to downtown and located between a coffee shop and a cheesy massage parlor. Maria hated the massage parlor. She thought it was tacky and ruined the charm of the street. Darlene usually liked to watch to see how many guys went in there. She swore it was a front for some hookers.

Darlene parked her car and headed toward the bookshop. She could already tell no one was in the store. She walked inside and waved to Maria.

"Oh, I am so glad you are here!" Maria exclaimed when she saw Darlene. "I'll have to hire someone right away, but you and I will have to work extra in the meantime."

"No problem," Darlene replied, shoving her purse under the front counter.

Darlene worked here for almost four years. Maria was a good boss. She always treated Darlene with respect and even gave her an entire month off after her father passed away three years ago. She was an older Native American woman with a bushy head of white hair that she barely cared enough to run a comb through. She wore large glasses that looked like they were from the seventies. Her fashion left a lot to be desired. Maria seemed to put on whatever she grabbed first and didn't look twice in the mirror afterward. For instance, today she had on a blue shirt with an off-color green skirt and black shoes. Her earrings were painted octopuses she had probably made herself — she liked making crazy jewelry.

"So," Darlene asked. "What happened with Jacob?"

Maria scowled. "He comes into work high as a kite, stinking of weed. Starts rambling to me about how he was in the woods last night and *like, totally felt something, like, man*," Maria said, mimicking Jacob's slow tone. "He was an hour late on top of it. I can't have someone late, stinking of weed and scaring off the few customers I get each month… especially after the last incident."

"Yeah, that was a mess." Jacob had hit on one of their regular clients in such a crass manner that she had threatened never to return again.

"Anyway, thank you so much for covering. I'm going to head off now. One of the grandkids is having a birthday party. You'll be okay?"

Darlene cast a sarcastic glance around the empty bookstore. "Wow, I hope I can handle it."

Maria laughed and grabbed her purse, heading to the door before stopping. "Hey, how was your date?"

Darlene frowned. "A total mess."

"Sorry, love. Hang in there, okay?" Maria said before leaving.

Hang in there. Darlene sighed. She has been hanging in there for way too long. When was she going to get a grip on her own life again? She walked around the shop to make sure everything was in its proper place. Darlene knew it would be, of course. It wasn't as if they had a ton of customers come through.

Maria had the marketable books up front, which brought in some tourist traffic during the summer. The farther back in the store one went, the stranger the books became. Darlene ended up in the back again, like she always did. Maria kept the supernatural books back here — books about ghosts, werewolves, mermaids and all sorts of paranormal creatures. Darlene always felt drawn to these; she never knew why. As a kid, she liked to pretend to be a ghost hunter. Nowadays, she liked to watch terrible B-movies about ghosts.

She trailed her fingers along the spines, letting the musty old-book smell wash over her. Darlene stopped in front of one book about ghosts, pulling it off the shelf. She had just flipped it open to a random page when the tiny bell on the door jingled. Surprised, Darlene looked up.

A tall man in amazing shape walked in. He had brown eyes, a beard and scruffy hair and wore a leather jacket. Darlene found herself gawking at him. He was so handsome her knees turned to jelly.

"Hi!" she said, but her voice sounded too high pitched, like she was eleven. "Hi, sorry, back here." She walked up front to him.

"Hello," he said in a deep voice that sent shivers down her back.

"Hi," Darlene repeated and then tried to get a hold of herself. "How can I help you?"

"I'm lost. I'm trying to find Roman's Tavern."

Her eyes widened. "I don't know if it's open yet."

Was this guy a hardcore alcoholic? It was still early in the morning, and he wanted to find a bar. Roman's Tavern was the only bar in town that Darlene hadn't ever gone to. It brought in a wild crowd that made her uneasy. Any time she drove past it and saw the crazy partying in there, she realized how much she wanted to go and that scared her. She was never much of a partier.

The fact that such an overwhelming urge to go when she drove by made her nervous. What if she went and lost her head?

The cops were there often, breaking up fights. Bike gangs were always seen there. Sometimes, if she left work at closing time, she'd drive by it and hear the thumping music and smell the cigarette smoke. She thought about going in every time. What would happen? Would she get hurt? What if she was missing out on something?

To Darlene, Roman's Tavern represented a life she could jump into if only she wasn't afraid. But she *was* too afraid. Life as a hermit was too comforting.

"Do you know where I can find it anyway?" he asked.

"It's down the street. On the corner, kind of pushed back a bit. It has this rundown broken sign that you might see if you drive by it."

"Thanks a lot, Miss…"

"Darlene." She held out her hand.

He stared at it for a second and then shook it. "Idris. Thanks for the help. You guys sell books about ghosts?" He pointed to the book she was holding when he came in.

His hand was so warm that Darlene had to snap herself back to the conversation. Was he sick? Shouldn't he be resting instead of going to some bar?

"Yes," she managed to respond. "We have a supernatural section in the back. Ghosts, vampires, werewolves…the usual."

"Werewolves, huh?" he replied. "Okay, well, nice to meet you."

Before Darlene could say anything else, he was gone.

She stood there, clutching her book to her chest, thinking about the feeling of warmth from his hand. What in the world was that about?

If you enjoyed this sample then look for **Alpha Packed: A BBW Paranormal Shifter Romance - Book 1**.

Other Books by Darla Dunbar

- The Romeo Alpha BBW Paranormal Shifter Romance Series

- Romeo Alpha Blood Lines Romance Series

- The Alpha Feud BBW Paranormal Shifter Romance Series

- The Alpha Packed BBW Paranormal Shifter Romance Series

- The Daemon Paranormal Romance Chronicles

- The Leather Satchel Paranormal Romance Series

Get the latest update on new releases from the author at:

https://darladunbar.com/newsletter/

About the Author - Darla Dunbar

Darla has been interested in paranormal romance since she was a teenager in high school. It was then that she discovered she could fulfill her fantasies through her writing.

Observing people and human behavior in the area of romance has always been one of her favorite pastimes. Combining that with an overactive imagination is a sure fire way of coming up with interesting themes.

Connect with Darla Dunbar

I really appreciate you reading my book! Here are my social media coordinates:

Friend me on Facebook: https://www.facebook.com/darladunbar/

Follow me on Twitter: https://twitter.com/DarlDunbar

Check me out on Goodreads: https://www.goodreads.com/author/show/8425857.Darla_Dunbar

Subscribe to my newsletter: https://darladunbar.com/newsletter/

Visit my website: https://darladunbar.com/